Publish Your Book
the Easy and Inexpensive Way

a practical guide to reaching
more people with your story

P & L Publishing
& Literary Services

Publish Your Book the Easy and Inexpensive Way
Copyright © 2023 S. Eugene Linzey
All rights reserved.
Pictures from Pixabay; used with permission

ISBN: 9798373554220

You've thought about writing…
You've dreamed about it…

And now …
P&L Publishing & Literary Services can help you do something about it.

Contents

Welcome from the President 4
Writing your Manuscript 8
Editing Your Manuscript 12
Editing the Front Matter 17
Editing the Back Matter 18
Forms to Fill Out 20
Submitting your Manuscript 24
Formatting and Designing your Book 28
Putting your Book in Print 34
How Much does it Cost to Publish my Book? 38
Your Book is Published! 44
Frequently Asked Questions 46
Contact Information 50
What people are saying about P&L 51
Final Thoughts 54
INDEX 55

Welcome from the President

My name is Eugene Linzey, and I'm the president of P&L Publishing & Literary Services. My staff and I are here to turn your message into a book so it is available to people who want to read it . . . who need to read it.

What are your passions? What flows through your mind every week, if not every day? What do you wish people knew? What would you tell others if you had an audience?

By writing a book, you have an opportunity to impact hundreds . . . maybe thousands . . . of lives. Writing and publishing is your escalator to the world. But how do you even get started?

P&L Publishing & Literary Services was created in 2019 for four basic reasons.

1. Definitive information about publishing is hard to get.
2. Prices are too high.
3. Many companies won't communicate by phone, and it's difficult to resolve some issues by email.
4. Waiting many months to finish the job is too long.

Therefore, P&L was formed to give an excellent product at a much lower price and a lot faster than other companies. We also know that writers are more comfortable and feel more secure if they can talk with the people who publish their books.

We explain the process and spell out the fees up front, and our clients enter the publishing agreement with most questions answered.

But P&L's mission goes far beyond that.

Many folks have a desire to share their stories, their personal experiences, and their views on life. People are creative, and through their writings they open their readers to new dimensions. And since all our staff members are writers, we know how to make the publishing experience a pleasant one.

Reading informs, empowers, and enables people to learn about life, and writing provides the reading material. You'll be surprised about the impact your book will have on someone's life!

Our goal is to make your journey as satisfying and meaningful as possible. We want you to be 100% pleased with the process and the end product.

This booklet will answer many of your questions and introduce you to our staff. But you will most likely have other questions, so please feel free to email or call us at any time. If we're busy with a client, we will do our best to get back to you the same day.

Come with us on a journey of fulfilling your dream of publishing your story or your message. We're here to help.

S. Eugene Linzey, President
P&L Publishing & Literary Services

So, you want to write a book, but you don't know how to get started?

I understand because there's a lot to consider. This booklet will help dispel the mystery of getting your book published and out to your readers. As you read this booklet, keep these four concepts in mind.

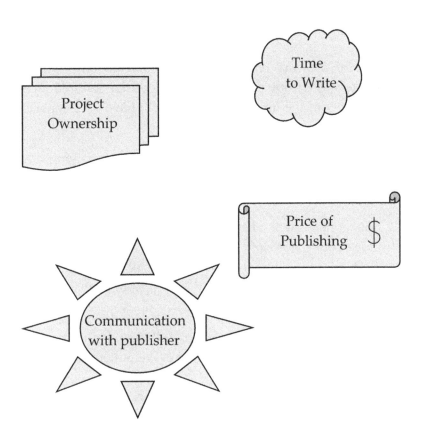

This booklet will introduce you to:

Writing your manuscript   Editing

Filling out forms   Formatting

Establishing the interior   Choosing a book cover

Creating eBooks   Marketing your book

Writing your Manuscript

Writing is an expression of who you are, what you believe, and what you want to accomplish. It demands an important investment of your time, resources, and talent. It takes time away from your family and friends. It may take up time that could be used for relaxation, vacation, or sleep. So make the best use of your time by writing well.

Step 1 – Choose a Comfortable Place to Write
Turn off attention-demanding electronics, including the phone. Give yourself time – no less than 10 minutes – to enter the correct frame of mind. Keep distractions to a minimum.

Step 2 – Develop a Writing Routine
Some folks write best in the morning while others prefer evenings or late at night. Some spend a week or two in a cabin in the hills to get away. Find the time and place that best suits you. Decide how you will progress. Some writers set a word count, such as 500 or 1,000 words at a setting. Others prefer a page or chapter count. The average word count for a novel is 90,000. So, if you can write 1,000 words in a setting (3 or 4 double-spaced, 8.5" x 11" pages with 1-inch margins will have about 1,000 words), you can write your book in 90 writing days.

Step 3 – Decide on a Theme
Most likely you have a topic in mind, and deciding on a theme will help keep you on track. If you are going to write about a historical event, steps 4-6 below might not be mandatory, but

they can certainly help. However, for a novel, these steps are crucial.

Step 4 – Design your Three Basic Sections

Create an idea for the beginning, middle, and end to the story. You want the beginning to give the reader background information related to the characters and the plot of the story. The middle will develop the main theme, and the end will provide a resolution of the plot. You might want to take a look at *Freytag's Pyramid* or Matthew Luhn's book, *The Best Story Wins* for helpful ideas.

Step 5 – Define your Characters

After you've decided on a theme for the book, consider which type of characters would be best suited for the story. Make a list of your proposed characters. Write a page about each one: who they are, what they are, and their importance to the story. Identify their strengths and weaknesses. Let your readers know what they look like and allow your characters to come to life on the page.

Step 6 – Draw on your Imagination

Your imagination is limitless. Keep it active when developing and writing your story. Even while writing a historical event, write it well with exciting, descriptive narrative.

Step 7 – Grab your reader's Attention

The first lines and the first chapter are crucial. George Orwell, writing the book, *1984*, began with, "It was a bright cold day in April, and the clocks were striking thirteen." That got people's attention! When you get stuck, save what you've got, and start on another idea in the book. However, the story often develops as you write. So start writing and let it flow! Make a habit of saving your work every 20 minutes. Saving your work can prevent a lot of frustration.

Step 8 – Give yourself Time to Write

Unless you are a professional writer with deadlines to make while earning large bonuses, do not crowd your calendar. Yes, you may have a deadline, but plan accordingly; give yourself time to relax and meet your deadline without getting stressed out.

There are a great many other ideas on the internet. Look up writers' groups. Join a writer's club. Interacting with other writers can be a great source of inspiration and encouragement.

Editing Your Manuscript

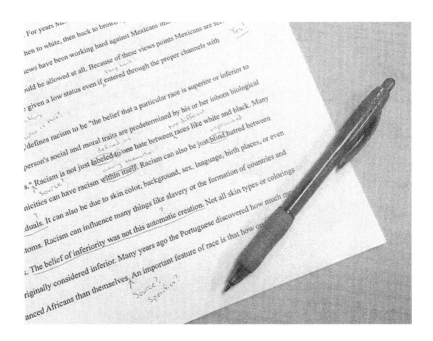

You've finally written it...
It's done ... it's over...
You are happy!

But there's a big question you've got to ask yourself. Is the book ready to fly or will it flounder? This is where many authors take a shortcut. They want to get the book out there and start making money right now. I know because I was one of them. But it doesn't always work that easily.

> A SECRET TO SUCCESS IS IN THE EDITING

You can be your own editor
Often, what someone tries to convey isn't what the reader perceives. That's why, after the document is completed, the author needs to become objective.
- ➤ **Take a break.** Put it down for an hour, or even walk away for a day or two. Returning with *fresh eyes* – with a more objective perspective – the author will see much that needs to be corrected or rewritten.
- ➤ **Read it aloud.** As your eyes see what your ears hear, you may identify incomplete or confusing sentences. You will spot missing or erroneous punctuation. You might find a paragraph that doesn't logically follow the preceding paragraph. You will probably find needless words and sentences. So modify anything that is either boring, doesn't make sense, or is unnecessary to the story.

> **Use your computer to help.** If your computer has the audio feature, have the computer read the document aloud as you follow. Stop it and revise the parts that don't sound right. If the computer doesn't have the audio program, ask your spouse or friend to read it to you.
> **Understand yourself.** We all have literary weaknesses, and it's sometimes difficult to identify them. Look for repeated words or phrases; unnecessary commas or semicolons; words that distract from the flow; idioms that may be misunderstood. Be ready to revise.

Sometimes more information needs to be added, so add it as you read. Add what's needed, delete what's unnecessary. Even the most talented writers set time aside to re-write. Very few authors have a flawless story on the first, second, third, or fourth draft.

Write, read, and rewrite. Make sure that you take the time to revise the story. Edit the document to the best of your ability, then be willing to ask a knowledgeable friend to review the manuscript for you.

Or you may need a professional editor

Sometimes the author is stuck and doesn't know what to do.

Marie called. She was distraught because she asked for and received advice from numerous friends about how to proceed. However, the advisors conflicted with each other and deepened her confusion. After we answered her questions and helped her understand what was involved, she hired P&L's editor who helped the message flow smoothly.

> Hiring an editor could prove to be a valuable investment

Editing takes time because the editor objectively reads every word. Depending on the genre, size of the book, and the level of editing the author requests, the process can take several days to a month. A good editor will not hurry because he/she wants to assure that your book is excellent. However, P&L's highly experienced editor endeavors to complete the job within two weeks.

Types of Editing P&L Offers

Proofreading: This process checks for typographical errors, punctuation, spelling, and grammar. Proofreading is applicable for a document that is almost ready for publication. Remember, another set of eyes can catch what the author's eyes miss.

Line Editing: This includes proofreading, but adds sentence repair, correction of wordiness, awkward word order, lack of clarity, flow of narrative, and more. Line editing polishes the document to a professional level.

Tips/Mentoring: You can always feel free to contact P&L with questions and comments. As time allows, we will offer tips and counsel by phone or email at no charge to help the author proceed with the project.

Be sure to plan your schedule to give the editor time to make your document great. This kind of work is done best without pressure.

Editing the Front Matter

Front matter is everything found prior to the main body of the book. Although only the title page, copyright page, and the ISBN are required, most books include several of the following components:

> Half title page
> Title page
> Copyright page
> Dedication
> Table of Contents
> Foreword
> Preface
> Epigraph
> Introduction
> Acknowledgements
> List of figures & tables
> Library of Congress #
> ISBN
> Map or Sketch

Self-publishing authors usually don't need to register the book with the Library of Congress. But if you have any questions about this, feel free to call us and ask about it.

Every book needs a barcode if the author plans on selling the book in stores. The codes can be purchased for prices starting at $25, or Amazon will provide them for no charge if using the KDP/Amazon system.

When thinking about what to include in your book, look at other books in your genre and see what they have. Different genres have preferences of what is included, but you'll find differences in books in the same field. Your editor or formatter can help you decide what is best for your book.

Editing the Back Matter

Back matter is everything found after the main body of the book. Although some books have no back matter, you'll often find some of the following; but the genre, topic, and author's desires are the deciding factors of what's included.

Endnotes	Postscript
Glossary	Epilogue
Bibliography	Acknowledgements
List of contributors	Index
Index	Conclusion
Author Biography	Other books by author
Appendix	Chapter title of next book

Back matter is optional, but some items are included in most books. It's important because some forms of back matter enhance, explain, or supplement the main text. Though usually found in nonfiction books, back matter can also enhance the appeal of fiction.

As you will do with front matter, think about what your readers may want to know. Providing appropriate information often enhances the value of the book.

Forms to Fill Out

Account Setup

The author will need to create an Amazon account. After that, using the same information, create a Kindle Direct Publishing (KDP) account. KDP will use the same Amazon log-in information because Amazon owns KDP. Both of these accounts are free.

Because KDP asks for sensitive information, the P&L staff cannot create this account for you. We will never ask for your banking information or your Social Security number. Of course, you are welcome to contact us if you have any questions, and we can guide you through that process. If you do not have an Amazon account, we'll send you the Jumpstart document upon your request. The directions are stated in a step-by-step format.

If you already have an Amazon account, you'll use the same login and password to set up a KDP account. Having the KDP account accomplishes several things.
1. This authorizes P&L to access your account and upload your finished book.
2. It allows the author to be paid when someone buys books online.
3. Online sales taxes are handled by Amazon.

P&L does not handle bank information or social security numbers, so setting up the account is done by the client. But, as stated previously, we can guide and give advice.

Service Agreement

This is the contract the client makes with P & L Publishing & Literary Services. It includes client's name, address, email, title and the description of book. It states whether or not the client wants us to make a book cover and what kind, whether the client wants a print, eBook, or both, the agreed upon price, how the client will pay P&L for the work, and a few other basic details. Most importantly, it authorizes us to represent you and your book in KDP.

Formatting Decisions

This form is where the author specifies the details of the book, and how it is to be set up in Amazon. Both P&L and the author need this information in writing to reduce potential misunderstanding.

We do not start work on the manuscript until these forms are completed and payment is received.

```
     Please fill in the blanks and answer all items for Kindle Direct Publishing.
  You are welcome to send an email with all your selections, if that works better for you.

  Paperback Details

  1.  Language _____

  2.  Book Title _____

  3.  Subtitle (optional) _____

  4.  Series Information (optional)
      Series Name _____
      Series Number _____

  5.  Edition Number (optional) _____

  6.  Author Information
         Title (optional) _____
      First Name _____
      Middle Name or Initial (optional) _____
      Last Name _____
      Are there any co-writers or contributors? If so, list their names.
```

Submitting your Manuscript

> In order to keep our prices at a low level, please send manuscripts to P&L by email as Microsoft Word documents.
> All manuscripts must be edited, correct, and complete prior to submitting to P&L for final formatting and uploading for printing. However, P&L has editors on staff if needed. See pages 15 and 42 for more information.

Although the book cover will normally be color, the default interior is black & white. If the author desires color inside the book, we can do that. Adding color to the interior of the book will not affect P&L's fees, but color will substantially increase the printing cost and the retail cost. Nevertheless, P&L will endeavor to accommodate the author's wishes.

Here are several quick tips to remember:
1. Up to 20 pictures or images can be included at no charge, but do not add them to your manuscript. If you want pictures in the book, please send them to P&L in a separate document and identify where each one is to be placed.
2. The manuscript should be typed, double-spaced, on 8.5"x11" pages, with 1" margins around.
3. Do not put section breaks or page breaks in your document. The formatter will do that.
4. Identify each chapter and chapter heading.
5. Do not use the tab key or the space bar to indent paragraphs and sentences.
6. Do not put two spaces between sentences.

7. Please do not attempt to add any formatting or "personal touches" to the document. Notify us of your desires and we'll add it.
8. Do not make any peripheral notes in your manuscript. If there is something you want us to know, tell us in an email or separate word document.
9. Chapters usually start on the odd-numbered page (right side) unless the author specifies otherwise.

Many book sizes are available. The size depends on the author's preference. As examples, we've published:
1. Bible study books with 425 pages in 7" x 9" format
2. Family memoirs with 490 pages in 6" x 9"
3. Short stories and testimonial booklets in 5" x 8"
4. Children's books with 36 pages in 8.5 " x 8.5"
5. The book in your hand is 5.5" x 8.5".

NOTE: Designing and formatting children's books and recipe books are more detailed, more complex, and requires more planning. Please discuss price with P&L.

If the author desires a logo or emblem with each chapter title, that will not count against photo or image count. We offer many options for creating a book from your manuscript. Feel free to discuss your ideas with P&L.

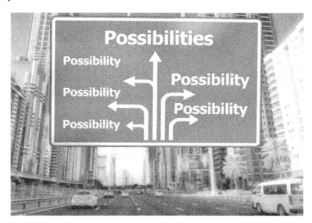

Formatting and Designing your Book

The next step is Formatting the Book for Publishing

If you would like assistance in designing and formatting to a high standard by professionals who care about quality, P&L Publishing & Literary Services may be the people to talk to. You'll be glad to know that P&L has a great reputation for its author-friendly, relational style of doing business and their low prices

> You may contact us at
> 14708 Oak Crest Dr.
> Siloam Springs, AR 72761
> (479) ~~270-1749~~ 228-3627
> email us at:
> plpubandlit2@gmail.com
> for a free consultation
>
> or look us up on our web sites:
> plpubandlit.org
> genelinzey.com

When you call, you will speak with a live, breathing, friendly person.

Meet the P&L Publishing & Literary Services Team

We are award-winning authors and journalists, conference speakers, mentors, and editors. We have advanced degrees or certifications and are trained to format and edit your manuscript to get it ready to publish.

Eugene Linzey, President
Lead Formatter

Vera Nelson
Chief Editor

Paul Linzey, Founder
Basic Cover Design

Grant Bell
Advanced Cover Design

Designing the Cover

Some of our clients are artists, others are photographers. Both present us with pictures or photos that they would like to have as book covers, and they turn out beautifully. The fact we always keep in mind is...

> The cover needs to grab the reader's attention

The color scheme and image need to, in some way, convey or support the message contained in the book. Our team has a track record of satisfying our clients, and we can apply the same standard of quality to your book.

If you have a good photo, a picture, or an idea for a cover, we'll use it if at all possible. As an example, an author in New Mexico offered a photo of a beautiful scenery to use for his cover. When he saw his finished product, he said, "I never knew my picture was that beautiful! It's prettier on the book than it is as a photo."

In addition to a formatting fee, many companies charge a minimum of $89 for a basic cover, over $200 for what is called a standard cover, and $800 or more for a deluxe cover. But P&L does not. If you would like P&L to create a cover, we'll do that for you. The basic cover is included in our low fee. But some others want a specialized cover. Our graphic design expert will do that for only $300, or you may find your own cover creator. We have the expertise to use your ideas and make a beautiful and meaningful cover for both front and back of the book.

Formatting the Interior

There are many ways to design or format the interior of the book. If the client doesn't have a stated preference, P&L can make suggestions, but the decision will be up to the author. The goal is to present a book that will grab and keep the reader's attention. With the variety of formats to choose from, our authors have always been happy with the results.

P&L formats novels, memoirs, biographies, historical works, devotionals, poetry, and more. We can include up to 20 pictures or photos for no extra charge. (There may be a charge for each additional photo). The formatted document is sent to the client for review and approval prior to publishing.

P&L also formats children's books, cookbooks, and other complex works. If a book such as these requires a specialized layout there may be an additional fee, but it will still be substantially lower than you'll find elsewhere. After a one-on-one consultation, you will be informed of the price before you make the decision to sign the service agreement.

A lot of people prefer reading on cell phones and other electronic devices. We can create an eBook for you, and at a substantial discount, P&L will produce both print and eBook at the same time. However, if the eBook is created more than 30 days after publication of the print book, the discount will not be applicable.

Approving Your Project

The author will have the opportunity to fully review the formatted document for approval prior to publishing.

1. P&L will email the project as a PDF file to the author.
2. The author will review every word to see if any errors have been made, or to see if any changes need to be made.
3. If errors are found, the author will list them and notify P&L, and we will correct them.
4. If the author wants to make changes, corrections, or revisions, we are willing to accommodate the author's wishes, but there may be an additional fee for the additional work. (See top of page 25.)
5. When the author approves the document, P&L will upload the work into KDP/Amazon.

Putting your Book in Print

The book is now written and edited. You're happy with the formatting. What's next?

You still have several decisions to make. These will be easy, but, nevertheless, they are important. Keep in mind that the author owns the manuscript and hires P&L to transform it into a book. But the author never loses ownership.

We are a company that works with you by preparing and submitting your manuscript to KDP/Amazon. When someone buys your book online, the order is farmed out to a regional publisher who prints and binds the book and then mails it to the buyer. This process is called Print on Demand (POD).

Keep in mind, Amazon and P&L do not stockpile books. But you, the author, may order up to 999 copies at a time and have them ready-to-sell at your convenience. Authors have the only "warehouse."

The Price of Your Book

Several factors are involved in pricing your book. These factors include the number of pages, what kind of book it is, the notoriety of the author, who the audience is, and more.

Authors should consider the price of other books in their chosen genre and know who their target audience is. A big mistake an author can make is setting the price too high. But setting the price too low might lead some people to think the book is not worth much. The author needs to find the balance.

Name-recognition has a bearing on price. If the author is well-known, the books often sell like hotcakes at higher prices.

In considering retail pricing, we also take into account the author's cost and Amazon's minimum allowable selling price.

Amazon determines the printing cost based on the number of pages in the book. This is the price the author buys the book for. Royalties are calculated at the listed price of the book, minus the print cost, times 60%. Amazon keeps 40%.

When ordering multiple copies, the price and royalty per book remain the same, but shipping and taxes vary. In one example, when the author ordered 1 copy of her family memoir, the shipping was $3.59, but when she ordered 12 copies, the shipping was $10. That averaged 83 cents per book which raised her profits when she personally sold the books.

When authors buy their own books at their author's price, there are no royalties. The profits are made when the authors sell them. A higher profit can usually be made when authors sell the books than when books are ordered online.

EBooks are handled differently. The price set for eBooks is usually half the price, or less, of the equivalent print book, and everyone, including the author, pays the same price. Royalties are paid for every eBook sold.

Pricing is important for both print books and eBooks. Pricing too low reduces its perceived value and credibility, and selling too high can often turn readers away. Again, the author needs to find the balance in pricing.

Do your homework and see what other books in your genre are selling for. P&L cannot set your price, but they can offer information about current prices.

Authors can sell from their own website, blog, or even by using a credit card reader and app on their phone or tablet.

How Much does it Cost to Publish my Book?

Publishing Options

There are three types of publishers in America: traditional, hybrid, and self-publisher. <u>All three require the author to be actively involved in marketing and selling the book after it's published.</u>

With a traditional publisher, there is no cost to the author after the manuscript is prepared and submitted. The publisher takes the risk, pays for the process, and owns the book. The author will get a small royalty for each book sold, but basically, the publisher owns all the rights to the book, and makes all decisions, including the title, the cover, and the price. Because the publisher takes the risks, they are highly selective as to what projects they are willing to accept. With 5,000 books published a day in America, traditional publishers want authors who are already well-known with a huge following so they can guarantee selling books to cover costs and make a profit.

Hybrid publishers have high prices and require the author to pay some of the expenses for producing the book. Some hybrid publishers require the author to buy a certain number of books. Either way, there is a significant cost to the author to publish this way. However, there are some benefits. Check them out.

Self-publishing is the third option, and has quickly become the preferred way to go for many reasons. The costs are lower, the process of publishing is quicker, and normally the author retains full ownership of the book even after uploaded for sale.

Most people who want to publish their book aren't famous, don't have a huge following, and might not have thousands of dollars to spend on producing their book. And self-publishing doesn't have to be super expensive.

Keep in mind that working through P&L, the author is always in control. You make every decision and also make a higher profit when you sell the book. However, you do have to be intentional about marketing the book and getting the word out. But we can give you some pointers on that.

We recommend that you shop around. Compare prices of different companies that help you self-publish. We think you'll find P&L to be among the better, lower-priced companies to do business with.

Self-publishing costs less, is faster, and the client retains ownership.

In all publishing options, the author bears the major responsibility of promoting the book. But the self-publishing author makes the decisions, sets the price, receives higher royalties, and the book can usually be published in less than a month ... sometimes, in less than two weeks.

A report came out in March of 2022 that the average cost for self-published books is about $2,000, and it can take a month to get the job done. Preparing an eBook is on top of that. But it's difficult to get prices from self-publishing companies because they don't want to scare potential clients away by the amount they charge. Instead, they tell us that they cannot give a price until we give them sufficient information. And in their situation, they are correct because their price depends on many factors; each factor has an additional cost.

But you'll like working with P&L Publishing & Literary Services. We put it all together and openly declare our fees up front. We tell you what the job will cost and there are no hidden fees to surprise you. Then we endeavor to get the job done in a couple of weeks.

The only reason our fee could change is if the client requests a modification in the service agreement, formatting decisions, or wants to change the document after substantial work has been completed.

Therefore, we request that the author complete and edit the manuscript – or hires an editor to finish it – prior to submitting it to the formatter, and doesn't request any substantial changes after that. (For your assistance, P&L has an editorial staff. See next page.)

Once the completed document has been placed in the P&L formatter's hands, and no changes are requested, finishing and uploading the book can often be done within a week.

P&L's Simple Fee Structure

Proofreading: $2.50 per page
The P&L editor checks for typographical errors, punctuation, spelling, and grammar. Proofreading is applicable for a document that is almost ready for publication. Remember, another set of eyes can catch what the author's eyes miss.

Line or Copy Editing: $5.00 per page
This procedure includes proofreading, but adds sentence repair, correction of wordiness, awkward word order, lack of clarity, flow of narrative, and more. Line editing polishes the document to a professional level.

Formatting Your Print Book: $500
- **For $500 you can have your book (100-500 pages) ready to print within a few days.**
    - $300 for less than 100 pages
    - $750 for 501-800 pages
- Our trained, award winning team will work to make your book look great.
- Basic Cover Design is included.
- If the author desires an advanced cover design, our graphic designer will charge a $300 fee, or you may hire another graphic designer to provide the cover image.

Formatting Your eBook: $500
- Many people prefer reading on their phone, tablet, or eReader.
- It makes sense, then, to offer your book digitally. The prices are the same as for the print book because both versions involve the same basic process.

Discount for Formatting both: $750
- We'll prepare your 100-500-page book in print <u>and</u> as an eBook and reduce the price for both from $1,000 to $750.
    - $400 for less than 100 pages
    - $1,100 for 501-800 pages
- Matching Basic Cover Designs are included.
- This discount applies if both the print book and eBook are requested during the initial project, or if requesting the eBook within 30 days of publishing the print book.

> The above prices include a book with up to twenty (20) photos or images, but please be aware that not all images are compatible with an eBook.
> P&L will work with you on that.

Your Book is Published!

You studied your topic. You lived it for months – if not years – as you wrote the book. You know the subject matter. You know the characters in the story better than anyone else in the world. Now, people need to hear about it.

You are the expert, so tell people about the book. One of our clients told folks wherever he went about his upcoming book. Many of them caught the excitement and prepaid for their copy. By the time his first order of books arrived, most were already sold!

You wrote the book, you got it published, you're the expert, now be your best sales agent.

Marketing Your Books

Now comes the promotional efforts.

Because the publishing world has changed the way it does business, traditional publishing companies normally do not accept clients who will not or cannot market their own books. In fact, many traditional companies won't accept authors unless they are already well-known and successful. To be accepted, clients must agree to numerous stipulations, which are often difficult to meet, and carry most of the burden of getting the message to the world.

> Self-publishing and hybrid companies are not set up to market books. P&L Publishing & Literary Services does no marketing.

P&L suggests the use of email, blog, Facebook, other social media, and person-to-person interaction to get the word out. Using the person-to-person method, a client in Arkansas earned over $400 in his first book-signing event.

An author in Alabama was a guest on a live broadcast and sold several thousand books in one weekend. Several of our authors have had TV or radio interviews, others have a weekly blog, social media, and they write newsletters. They all produce results.

You also may want to give a book away for free once in a while to someone who has a social outlet (radio, TV, blog, church, newspaper, etc.). The possibilities are endless. The main thing is to tell others about your books in every method you can think of. It can be done ... it is being done.

Frequently Asked Questions

Does P&L Publishing & Literary Services print books?

No. We assist the author in preparing the work to be published. The author retains ownership of the work in every stage of the process and is welcome to interact with P&L in every step. It is KDP/Amazon who selects the printer for each book order.

Who edits the books?

The author is the writer and the primary editor. However, if the client desires an editor to help in the final writing stage, P&L has professional editors on staff to help. The editorial fees are found on page 42, but please feel free to call us for more information. (Contact info is on pages 29 & 50.)

What does print on demand mean?

P&L uploads the work into KDP/Amazon which has contracts with several great printers in the USA. When orders are placed, KDP sends the order to a printer who downloads the file. The books are printed and sent from the printer directly to the buyer. Thus, it is called Print on Demand (POD).

How do I get the document to you?

Send it to P&L by email or send it by US Mail on a thumb drive. (Contact info is on pages 29 & 50.)

I tried to put page numbers on the document, but it's not working right.

It's always important that you set up your document to automatically paginate. If you need help with this, give us a call. If you cannot do it, then our formatter will take care of that.

I prefer a font other than Times New Roman. Are you okay with that?

The standard font for submitting any manuscript to a publisher is Times New Roman size 12 font, with one-inch margins on top, bottom, and both sides. If you want the printed book to have a specific font, please say that in the formatting decisions form, and we'll make sure the book is prepared that way.

May I use the Tab key or space bar to indent paragraphs?

No. Always set your document to automatically indent new paragraphs. If you need help, ask someone to show you how to do that.

How can I order books at the author's price?

After the book is uploaded and ready for sale, you'll find a button in your Amazon account that starts the simple process. Just follow the directions. If requested, P&L will send the detailed steps to authors after the books are uploaded.

Are there any books you won't accept?

Yes. P&L reserves the right to refuse to format, edit, or publish for any reason whatsoever, including but not limited to, what we believe: (1) is false, misleading, or defamatory; (2) is offensive, abusive, or uncivil in tone; (3) is harmful, threatening, or intimidating; (4) contains profanity, hate messages, or personal attacks against others; (5) impersonates another person or misrepresents your affiliation with a person or entity; (6) violates another person's or entity's intellectual property rights, publicity, privacy rights, or other legal rights; (7) is otherwise inappropriate or undesirable.

How do I put photos in my document?
Send the photos (JPEG or PNG) to P&L. Identify the page where each photo is to be placed, and we'll be happy to place up to 20 in the document. There may be an additional fee for more than twenty pictures.

Can I make changes in my book after it's published?
Yes. Working with P&L, you never lose ownership of your book, and you can ask for changes even years later. But if the request is made after publication, there will be an additional fee.

If I call P&L, will I talk to a machine?
No. You'll speak with a real live person. However, if we are not available when you call, please leave a message and a phone number, and we will endeavor to return the call the same day. We are people-oriented, and we intend to please our clients.

Do I need an agent to go through your company?
No. Email us at plpubandlit2@gmail.com or look us up at plpubandlit.org. You'll deal directly with us.

How long will it take to get my book published?
Once the formatter starts working on the manuscript, he usually will have it completed and back to the author for approval in less than a week. If the author does not request changes, the manuscript can be uploaded into the Amazon/KDP system within 24 hours of the approval. It then enters the Amazon 72-hour review. If all goes well, the book can be ready for purchase in less than two weeks after the P&L formatter starts on the project.

Contact Information

This booklet presents a summary of what you need to know about writing and getting your book into the hands of readers. There is much more to know, however, so please feel free to call, write, or email us. Contact info is found below.

It will be our joy to help your dream of becoming an author come true. You'll find us easy to work with.

> Contact Info:
> P&L Publishing and Literary Services
> 14708 Oak Crest Dr.
> Siloam Springs, AR 72761
> (479) ~~270-1749~~
> 228-3627
> plpubandlit2@gmail.com
> Web: plpubandlit.org
> Web: genelinzey.com

What people are saying about P&L

My book looks wonderful. It is far more beautiful and professional than I ever imagined it would be. You guys have been such a blessing to me. Thank you for all you have done.

Rachel, Alabama

I never thought I would actually see my writing in print, and the cover is beautiful! Thank you.

Chuck, New Mexico

I never thought it would be this inexpensive getting my book in print. My order of 50 books came in and nearly sold out the first week. I've got to order more already. Thank You! By the way, I've already told others to call you to publish their books.

Charles, Arkansas

I can't believe how quickly you got my book ready for sale. I have at least three more I'm going to write, and I want you to do it for me.

Pat, Missouri

I finally have my book ready to give to my Grandkids. Thank you for your friendship and your professionalism.

Tom, Oklahoma

I'm amazed at how you made my book look so good. You even used my old photo and made it look good. Thank you! I have 2 more books I'm working on, and I'll come to you.

R.C., Arkansas

I must say, this book really looks good. You did a great job. Thank you again because without all this wonderful assistance, I would still be agonizing over what to do. There is no way I could have done this without you.

Brenda, Texas

Hey, it looks GREAT! Thanks, you're the best!

Brook, Florida

Wow! Thank you so much for taking my manuscript and turning it into a great book.

Stan, Arkansas

A friend came over today, and we had a glass of wine with cheese and crackers to celebrate! I'm still so excited. Now my book has sold internationally! I feel almost famous.

Nancy, Florida

The print-on-demand and the eBook look great! Thank you so much. I appreciate all the work you invested in helping me get the project completed.

Tim, North Carolina

In awe of how beautiful it turned out! We are both pleased with all aspects of your publishing services. Thank you!

Alice, Michigan

I love it! We could not have accomplished this book without your expertise. More than 6,000 sold in the first month! Thanks again for all your help!

Jan, Georgia

Oh, my Lordy sakes! We're in love with the book! It looks beautiful. Thanks so much for what you did for us!

Ann, Florida

Final Thoughts

Thank you for considering P&L Publishing & Literary Services. We hope this information has been helpful because it's our desire for you to make meaningful and educated decisions when you publish your book – or books.

So please call us, email us, or look us up on our website. We'll talk with you and do our best to answer all your questions.

INDEX

A
Account Setup 21
Approving the Project 33
Audio Reading 14
Author's Price 36

B
Back Matter 18
Barcode 17
Be your own Editor 13
Blogs 37, 45
Book Covers 31, 42, 43
Book is Published 6, 44

C
Children's Books 26, 32
Client Approval 33, 50
Color in the Book 25, 31
Computer Reading 14
Contact Information 29, 50
Copyright 2, 17
Cost to Print 36, 42, 43
Cost to Publish Books 38, 41
Cover Design 30, 31, 42, 43

D
Decide on a Theme 8
Define Characters 9
Design Basic Sections 9
Designing the Book 28
Designing the Cover 31
Discount in Formatting 43

Develop Writing Routine 8
Draw on Imagination 9

E
EBooks 7, 32, 36
Editing Back Matter 18
Editing Front Matter 17
Editing the Manuscript 12, 30, 33
Editor 13-17, 30, 41-42, 48
Examples of Books Published 26

F
FAQs 47
Final Thoughts 55
Fonts 49
Formatting
    Decisions 22, 35, 39, 40, 41, 49
    eBook Price 32-36, 40-43
    Print & eBook price 35-37, 40, 42
    Interior 25, 32
    Options 26, 39-40

Print Book Price 35-36, 43
Forms to Fill Out 20, 22
Front Matter 17-18

G
Getting Started 6
Allowing Time to Write 10
Grab Reader's Attention 10, 32

H
Hiring an Editor 14-15
Hiring a Cover Maker 31, 39, 42
Hybrid Publishers 39

I
Imagination 9
Interior Design 25, 32
Interior Formatting 25, 32
ISBN 17
Items in Front Matter 17
Items in Back Matter 18

L
Library of Congress 17
Line Editing 15
Line Editing Price 42

M
Marketing Your Books 39, 40, 45
Major topics in Book 7
Meet the P&L Staff 30
Mentoring 15

O
Options 26, 39, 40
Ordering Books 35, 36, 49

P
P&L's Price Structure 42-43
P&L Staff 30
POD 35, 48
Possibilities 26, 45
President's Welcome Letter 4
Price of Printing 25, 36, 42-43
Price of Publishing 38-39, 41
Price of Your Book 35-36

Professional Editor 14, 48
Project Ownership 26, 35, 40, 48
Proofreading 15, 42
Proofreading Price 42
Publishing Options 39-40
Putting the Book in Print 34-35

R
Review 32, 33, 50
Revise 14
Rewrite 14

S
Secret to Success 13, 45
Self-Publishers 39
Self-Publishing 17, 39-40, 45
Selling Books 17, 36-37, 39
Service Agreement 21, 32, 41
Shipping 36
Social Media 45
Submitting the Manuscript 24, 25, 41, 48

T
Table of Contents 3
Tips/Mentoring 15, 25
Tips to Remember 25
Traditional Publishers 39, 45
Types of Books P&L Publishes 4, 32
Types of Editing 15

U
Using your Imagination 9

W
What People say about P&L 51
Welcome Letter 4

When P&L was Started 29
Writing the Manuscript 8

Y
Your Book is Published 44
You've Written it 13

Made in the USA
Monee, IL
04 August 2023

40432536R00036